For Kate McMullan
and with gratitude, always, to Anne Schwartz
— M. P. O.

For Kier, Chlöe, Dad and Mom
— G. P.

Author's Note

As I reworked the story of "Jack and the Beanstalk," I studied many versions of the familiar tale, but the retelling that most inspired me was Andrew Lang's "Jack and the Beanstalk," from *The Red Fairy Book*, published in 1890.

According to Iona and Peter Opie in *The Classic Fairy Tales*, the original written source for virtually all early retellings of "Jack and the Beanstalk" was Benjamin Tabart's publication, *The History of Jack and the Bean-stalk, Printed from the Original Manuscript, Never Before Published*, 1807.

ALADDIN PAPERBACKS
An imprint of Simon & Schuster Children's Publishing Division
1230 Avenue of the Americas, New York, NY 10020
Text copyright © 2000 by Mary Pope Osborne
Illustrations copyright © 2000 by Giselle Potter
All rights reserved, including the right of reproduction
in whole or in part in any form.
ALADDIN PAPERBACKS and colophon are
trademarks of Simon & Schuster, Inc.
Also available in an Atheneum Books for
Young Readers hardcover edition.
Designed by Angela Carlino
The text of this book was set in Packard.
The illustrations for this book were rendered in
pencil, ink, gouache, gesso, and watercolor.
Manufactured in China

First Aladdin Paperbacks edition October 2005
20
The Library of Congress has cataloged the hardcover
edition as follows:
Osborne, Mary Pope.
Kate and the beanstalk / by Mary Pope Osborne ;
illustrated by Giselle Potter.—1st ed.
p.   cm.
Summary: In this version of the classic tale, a girl climbs to the
top of a giant beanstalk, where she uses her quick wits to outsmart
a giant and make her and her mother's fortune.
ISBN-13: 978-0-689-82550-7   ISBN-10: 0-689-82550-1 (hc.)
[1. Fairy tales. 2. Folklore—England. 3. Giants—Folklore.] I. Potter,
Giselle, ill. II. Jack and the beanstalk. English. III. Title.
PZ8.O815Kat 2000 [398.2]—dc21 99-27029
ISBN-13: 978-1-4169-0818-0   ISBN-10: 1-4169-0818-8 (Aladdin pbk.)
0719 SCP

Kate

and the Beanstalk

Written By
Mary Pope Osborne

Illustrated By
Giselle Potter

An Anne Schwartz Book

Aladdin Paperbacks
New York London Toronto Sydney

Long ago, a girl named
Kate lived with her mother in a
humble cottage. One day, after a hard
winter, Kate's mother was in despair.

"We are sure to die from hunger," she said,
"unless we sell our only cow to get money for food."

Kate was a plucky girl who loved to help. "Don't worry," she
said, giving her mother a hug. "I'll take care of everything."

And she set out for market with their cow.

On the way, Kate met a beggar holding a small sack.

"Magic beans," the beggar said in a creaky voice.

"How extraordinary!" said Kate when she saw them, for the brown beans shone like dark gold. "I don't think I can live without them."

"They can be yours—in exchange for your cow," said the beggar.

Without another thought, Kate traded her cow for the beans and rushed home to give them to her mother.

But to Kate's surprise, her poor mother was horrified. "Our only hope is gone!" she cried. "Now we will surely starve!" And she tossed the beans out the window.

Hungry and forlorn, Kate went to bed.

During the night, Kate couldn't sleep. She got up and crept into the moonlit garden.

She gasped. For in the darkest corner, a giant beanstalk rose into the sky. It rose higher and higher and higher still, till it disappeared behind the clouds.

"Does it never end?" whispered Kate.

Without waiting for morning, Kate began climbing the beanstalk. She climbed and climbed and climbed . . .

. . . up and up and up and up.

When Kate reached the top, light was creeping into the gray sky. Through a misty haze, she saw the most astonishing sight: Above the clouds was a countryside with fine woods, a crystal stream, a rolling sheep meadow, and a mighty castle.

As Kate stared in wonder, an old woman hobbled out of the woods.

"Hello!" said Kate. "Is that castle your home?"

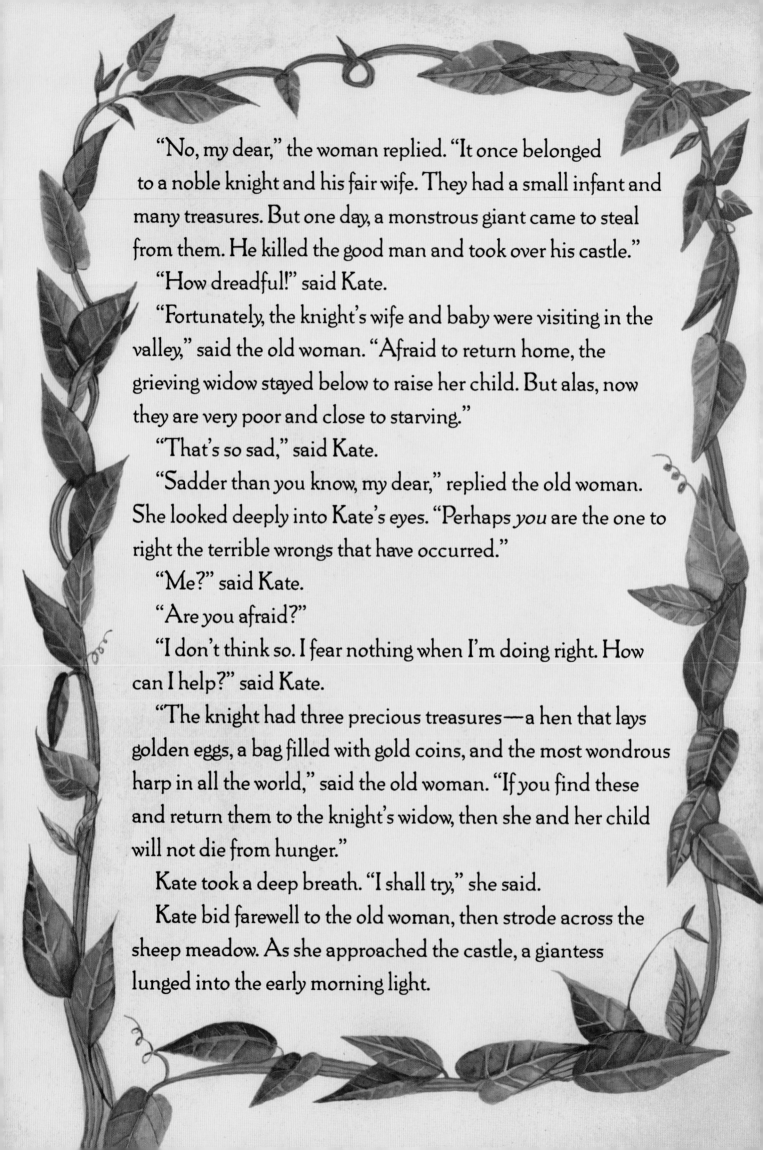

"No, my dear," the woman replied. "It once belonged to a noble knight and his fair wife. They had a small infant and many treasures. But one day, a monstrous giant came to steal from them. He killed the good man and took over his castle."

"How dreadful!" said Kate.

"Fortunately, the knight's wife and baby were visiting in the valley," said the old woman. "Afraid to return home, the grieving widow stayed below to raise her child. But alas, now they are very poor and close to starving."

"That's so sad," said Kate.

"Sadder than you know, my dear," replied the old woman. She looked deeply into Kate's eyes. "Perhaps *you* are the one to right the terrible wrongs that have occurred."

"Me?" said Kate.

"Are you afraid?"

"I don't think so. I fear nothing when I'm doing right. How can I help?" said Kate.

"The knight had three precious treasures—a hen that lays golden eggs, a bag filled with gold coins, and the most wondrous harp in all the world," said the old woman. "If you find these and return them to the knight's widow, then she and her child will not die from hunger."

Kate took a deep breath. "I shall try," she said.

Kate bid farewell to the old woman, then strode across the sheep meadow. As she approached the castle, a giantess lunged into the early morning light.

"Help me!" the huge woman roared. "My husband makes me cook from the cock's crow to the owl's hoot! Whenever I hire servants, he gobbles them up!"

"I'll be your servant," said Kate. "But you must hide me from the giant."

Kate helped the giantess make breakfast until the sun came up. When she heard the giant coming down the hall, she trembled with fear. His footsteps sounded like the booms of a cannon.

"Hide!" whispered the giantess, and she pushed Kate into a closet.

Peeking through the keyhole, Kate watched and listened.

"Fee, Fi, Fo, Fum'un,

I smell the blood of an Englishwoman.
Be she alive or be she dead,
I'll grind her bones to make my bread."

"Don't be silly," said the giantess. "You only smell the wagonload of bacon I fried for your breakfast."

"Oh," said the giant.

When the giant finished eating, he said, "Bring me the knight's hen."

The giantess brought out a small brown hen.

"Lay!" ordered the giant. And the little hen laid a golden egg.

"Ha-ha-haah!" roared the giant. "I love my lovely little stolen hen." Then he put down his head and fell asleep, snoring as loud as thunder.

Ever so quietly, Kate crept out of the closet.

She grabbed the hen and rushed from the castle. She ran across the sheep meadow to the beanstalk. Down and down and down she climbed and climbed and climbed, until she landed *kerplop* in the garden.

Kate sighed with relief. "It's better if Mother doesn't know of the danger I've been in," she whispered to the hen. "Stay here, until I can return you to the knight's poor widow."

Kate hid the hen behind a bush, then slipped back inside her house.

Kate knew she must disguise herself to return to the castle. That night she dressed in a wig and a beard, crept out to the moonlit garden, and climbed the beanstalk again.

Kate climbed and climbed and climbed . . .

. . . up and up and up and up.

In the light before dawn, Kate crossed the sheep meadow and knocked on the castle door.

When the giantess came out, she roared,

"Help me!

I need a servant! The last one stole our hen and ran away!"

All happened as before. Kate helped the giantess make breakfast until the sun came up. When they heard the giant's booming footsteps and bellowing voice, the giantess hid Kate in the closet.

"Fee, Fi, Fo, Fum'un,

I smell the blood of an Englishwoman.
Be she alive or be she dead,
I'll grind her bones to make my bread."

"Calm down," said the giantess. "You only smell the mountain of hash I made for your breakfast."

"Oh," said the giant.

When the giant finished eating, he said, "Bring me the knight's money bag."

The giantess brought out a bag filled with gold coins, and the giant greedily counted them.

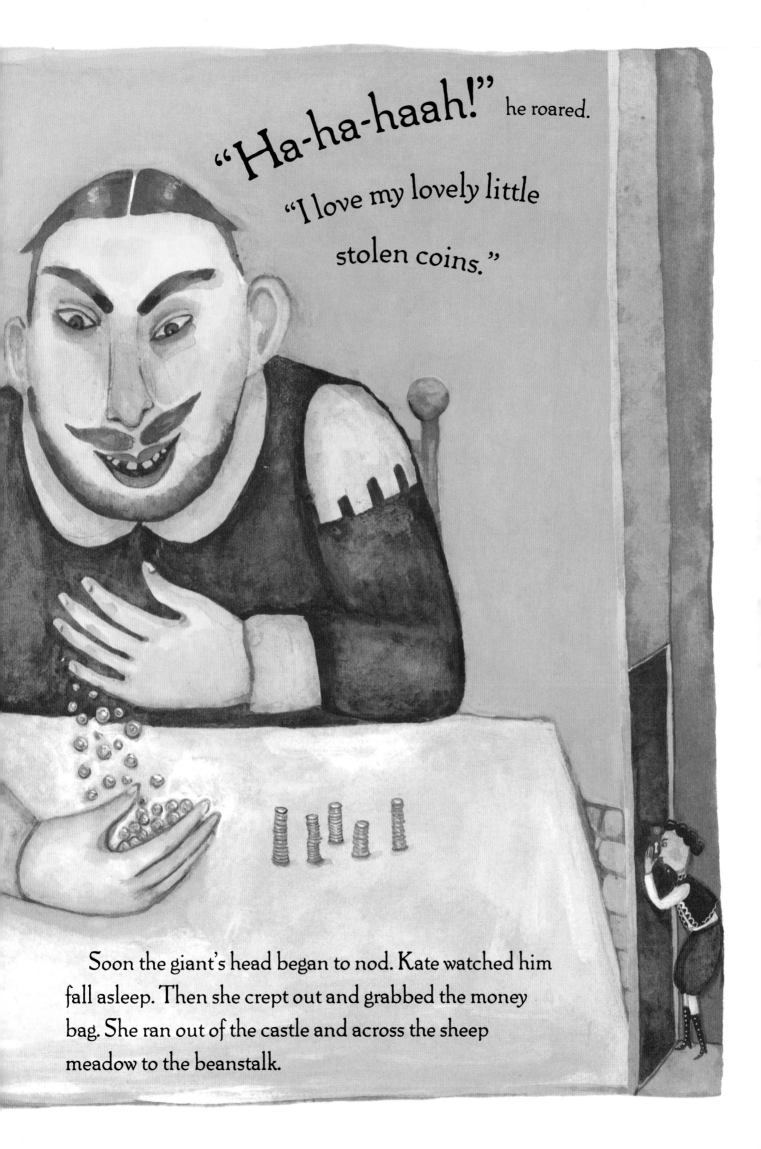

"Ha-ha-haah!" he roared.

"I love my lovely little stolen coins."

Soon the giant's head began to nod. Kate watched him fall asleep. Then she crept out and grabbed the money bag. She ran out of the castle and across the sheep meadow to the beanstalk.

Down and down and down . . .

. . . she climbed and climbed and climbed, until she landed
kerplop in the garden.

"Goodness!" said Kate. "What a day! I must hide these coins
until I can return them to the knight's poor widow."

Kate hid the money bag with the hen, then slipped back inside
her house.

That night, Kate disguised herself once again and started up the beanstalk.
She climbed and climbed and climbed ...
... up and up and up and up.

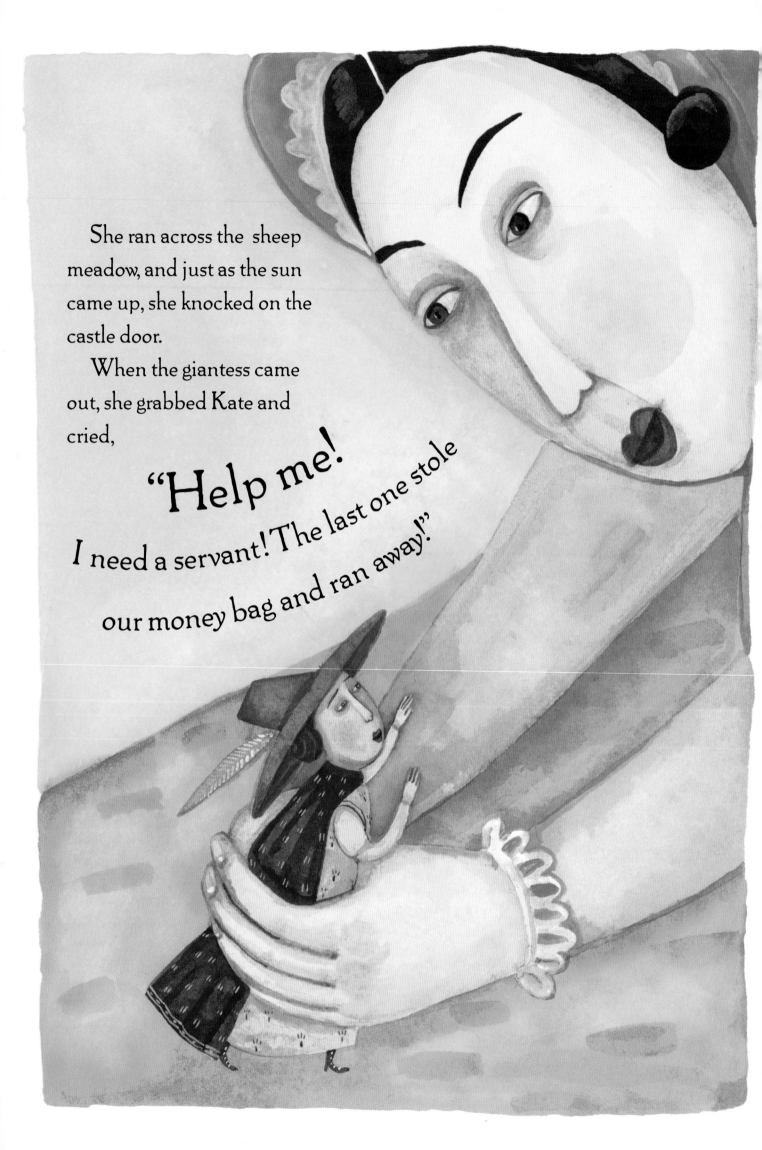

She ran across the sheep meadow, and just as the sun came up, she knocked on the castle door.

When the giantess came out, she grabbed Kate and cried,

"Help me! I need a servant! The last one stole our money bag and ran away!"

Again, all happened as before. Kate helped the giantess make breakfast. Soon the giant's footsteps boomed down the hall, and the giantess hid Kate in the closet.

"Fee, Fi, Fo, Fum'un,

I smell the blood of an Englishwoman.
Be she alive or be she dead,
I'll grind her bones to make my bread."

"You old fool," said the giantess. "You only smell the sea of fish soup I made for your breakfast."

"Oh," said the giant.

When the giant finished his soup, he cried, "Bring me the knight's singing harp."

The giantess brought out a magnificent harp, the only one of its kind in the world. The harp sparkled with diamonds and rubies, and it had strings made of gold.

"Sing!" bellowed the giant.

The harp began to sing a sad, haunting song. It sang of the past, of the noble knight, his lost wife and child, of golden days and starry nights. The harp's lovely song nearly broke Kate's heart.

When the giant fell asleep, she crept out from behind the door, seized the harp, and ran away with it.

But the harp was so frightened, it sang high, fearful notes: *"Help me! Help me! Help me!"*

"Quiet!" said Kate. "I'm going to return you to the knight's poor widow!"

But the giant had already been awakened. He jumped up and with a shout, he ran after Kate.

Kate flew like the wind across the sheep meadow. She grabbed the beanstalk and started down with the harp, the giant fast on her heels.

Down and down and down and down…

…she climbed and climbed and climbed, and the giant climbed and climbed and climbed right after her.

As soon as Kate's feet touched the ground, she shouted, "Mother! Bring the ax! Hurry!"

Kate's mother ran out with the ax, and Kate grabbed it.

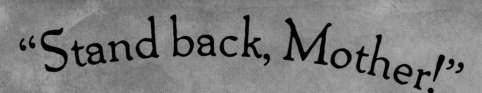

"Stand back, Mother!"
Kate cried.

With one mighty blow, Kate chopped the beanstalk in two. Down and down it fell, down through the sky, and down fell the giant— *WHUMP!*—down into the garden, breaking his neck. The ground shook like an earthquake.

Kate's mother took one look and cried out in horror, "That's the giant that killed your father!"

"My father?" asked Kate.

Before her mother could answer, a fairy approached in a chariot drawn by two peacocks.

"Greetings, brave Kate," she said. "As Queen of the Fairies, I have long wanted to avenge the treachery done to the good knight. But first I needed to know if his daughter was worthy of her inheritance. So I disguised myself as both the beggar and the old woman and sent you on your quest to your father's castle."

"My father's castle?" Kate looked at her mother, who nodded.

"I never spoke of your father after he was slain," Kate's mother said. "He would be most proud of you now."

Kate hugged her mother, and they wept for the sorrow and wonder of it all.

Then they climbed into the chariot and rose through the clouds, to the castle that was once again theirs...

...up and up and up and up.

Kate asked the giantess to stay on as their cook.

"Thank you for your kindness," said the
giantess. "Would you like a biscuit and jam?"

"Indeed," said Kate and her mother.

And the giantess served them a biscuit as big
as a cow.